Contheman... Shr00ve Head

Constantine O'Donnell

ISBN: 978-1-63950-239-4 (sc)
ISBN: 978-1-63950-240-0 (e)

Writers Apex

Gateway Towards Success

8063 MADISON AVE #1252
Indianapolis, IN 46227
+13176596889
www.writersapex.com

www.cacbethel.com
www.igoeministry.com

CONTENTS

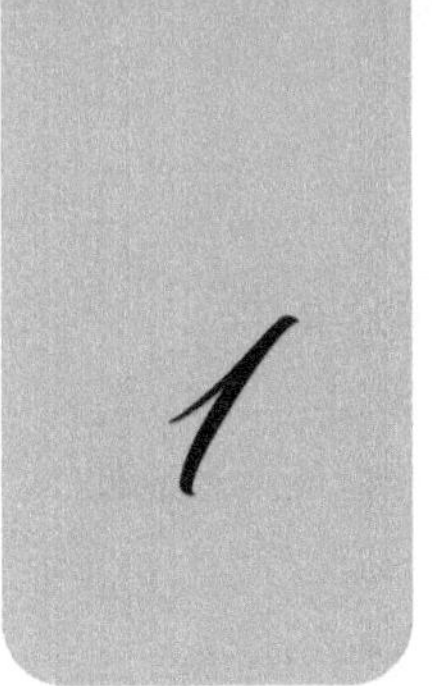

PAEDOPHILE PARK LOL

I have been sectioned once again. This time is the most ridiculous. I did not tidy my house. My mother reported me to the mental health services. She got me locked up. I am fucking fuming!!!

Anyway, I'm out of the little piece of shit cold house…it's fucking freezing!!! I am now in a warm mental asylum where everybody has been told to give me fucking respect!!! I'm going to start with a poem… my favourite to write.

Mental Asylum Shitbags

The nurses have such an ego,
They condescend every chance they get,
The Gardai are now starting at 50,
Every one of them will be a pet,
The Criminals are all laughing,
They can't bloody wait,
Get all their Daddy's in,
And run the fucking state,
McGregor is a fuckwit,

> He cannot even fucking fight,
> All those midget fighters he fights,
> Are not worth the shit off my prick,
> My Army of men and women,
> Are ready for me to have fame,
> They will all be in the sunshine,
> Enjoying my new Game!!!

My cousin Styley McC is one of my haters. He did not amount to anything in his life. He begrudges everything and everybody and is at a loss when you talk about the world.

My so-called friend Thomas Cock McLaughlin is a dumb fuck farmer from the hill. He married a woman that fancied the pants off me. When he was asking her out for a date, he asked me along with him. He used my presence and jokey charm to woo her into a false reality. That reality is one a few of my friends have used in the past to woo their women too. The women all think they'll be spending their lives hanging out with me. Not to be I'm afraid. These men are a bunch of dickheads. I now fly with people my own altitude. I learned it in Superyachting. A Captain told me it.

All my school friends are dead and gone. They all abandoned me when I was in need. I have a few friends in Ireland but the rest can go suck their mothers cock!!!

My secondary school days were pretty tame compared to my younger days at Greencastle national school…I had so much fun when I was very young!

My College days were the best…drinking, women and drunken antics!!! One day I was drinking in the morning before college when my roommate…a woman….offered me a blowjob. She'd only just moved in. I said fucking right! She got naked. Everyone else had gone to college.

She sat me on the couch and started sucking me off. I came in seconds and she took the beer that I was holding off me and smoothly put the cum into it. Then swirled it around and fucking sank it! I applauded her and gave her a passionate kiss on the lips. She pulled back and said "I just wanted to thank the Captain of the House for treating me like one of your own".

We had so much fun in the house. Firgrove park. I'm going to buy that house. It can be my Cork residence. So many good memories there.

My Head lecturer Viv Gough was a sarcastic comedian. He let us away with so much. There were a handful in our class and they were all wildmen. My best friend Daire was going through a change. The Shipping company he went with gave him a very bad attitude. The RTE...Irish television are on in the background as I am writing this. They just threatened me...totally innocuous to everybody else. They did a short documentary on Austin, Texas. It was a pre-emptive strike. They know from my Facebook I plan on moving there. The threat on RTE news was that the crew that went there warned all its women to beware of a Donegal man coming to woo all their women. They've told them I'm a wife beater and an asshole. This crap the Irish people all around the world are doing to me is going to end tourism on their little fucking rain drenched island. I will make sure of IT. And I will invite every ethnicity to this Island of rain and wind to bask in the clouds and weak sunshine...

The reason for the title SHROOVE HEAD is that it is where I come from and I'm the Boss man. Some there will refute that but they are just jealous. I'm the bloody boss.

My people all over the country have been kept in the dark about the gaslighting and abuse I have received over the last 20 years. These people are so smart at it, they know all my connections. They've been tapping my phone and reading my emails. They fucking try and dictate

to me in public. This fucking torrent of abuse is the most evil, sadistic…
coolest thing for inspiration. I am now British. I have a British passport
and I am putting my Irish passport in a museum. It will come to be
that anybody with an Irish passport will have restrictions when they
travel. They will not be allowed to do drugs in the new world and will
be tested with a new machine that can detect narcotics in the breath.
All they'll have to do is blow into the bag. The whole plane full of Irish
people will be warned - No Drugs! If they do not comply…they will
be confined to the Island of Ireland for life. One strike and you're out.

There will be no drugs on the Island of Ireland in 5 years time. That
means the whole Island…Northern Ireland included. Drugs will be
legal in every other country all over the world. This will be brought
into place when the aliens arrive on the 11th of April 2024. This book
will probably not be out then but this our pre-emptive strike. LOL.

I was once cliff climbing around Shroove head with my mate Connell.
His first name is Paddy but it's such a common name in Irish history…
I'm calling him Connell in all my writings. He's in a few good stories.
So then, his full name is Paddy Connell…

I asked my Dad when I was really young why he wasn't called Paddy
O'Connell? My Da as usual was very humorous. He said they lost the
"O" during the Famine because they stole a potato!!!

Connells father was a Guard. He inspired me to become an undercover
Guard when I was 8. I thought I won't tell anybody but I'll fight crime
on my own and people of this Earth…that is what I have done. All
over the world. Especially in Anitibes.

Connells father had lots of Garda friends. They were all a bit wild. I
used to love them. They loved hearing our tales of adventures around
the areas as kids…they always involved law breaking. They used to
howl laughing and when I was leaving their house to go home…the

both of his parents would shout "Be good!!!". My reply was "Always!!!". They used to howl laughing.

I've used it in Spain as well when women say it to me…"Siempre!!!". It means 'always' in Spanish.

The aliens are watching how I am treated in the mental asylum this time in. There is already some ugly bitches of nurses condescending me. I'm marking their cards. I have had so many headaches with their inadequate diversified crap.

As a King I am devoid of emotion for human life. A million people in the I.R.A are going to get Cancer. I laugh rather than cry. They have been so vicious on me. They have collectively made my life miserable for 20 years. There is 1 Billion of them altogether. They've been recruiting for 20 years to stop my career and my domination plans for the world. The U.V.F are now the terrorist group I support as a Brit!!!

My sister is the fucking bitch of the planet. She is the most spoiled girl I know AND what a fucking arrogant attitude she has. My brother Jailbird James who is 10 years younger than me is a hard fucking grafter. He is a professional body builder and a Captain and a Pilot. His wife is besotted with him. I think they are really well suited. Their kids will not be handicapped which I'm sure is a fear of my brothers. I have inside info the kids will be fine! His last girlfriend smoked so much hash and drank so much that she had an inhospitable womb. Their child that was conceived and died before birth was heavily spasticated. Thank fucking God it died in the womb. I was so relieved AND the only one in the family that was happy the spastic died lol. It would have ruined his life. He got away from Cassie who incidentally fancied me lol and came back from the dead to become one of the top Captains/Pilots in the world. I'm so proud to call him my younger brother and oh my God how smart are his children going to be? I'm so excited. Our kids will be around the very same age and I will have millions and millions of dollars to spend on everyone. The McGilloways…my cousins will be made very wealthy as well. The Dicksons are really funny people… also my cousins and are also going to be extremely wealthy. The cousins on my mothers side…the McLaughlins will all be rich by me as well.

My mother is so cruel. She locked me up even though I was about to be famous. I got in contact with the comedian Joe Rogan. He said he would be honoured to have me on the show. He is so cool!!! And intelligent. I want to have his babies. I told him I had no money so he said he would fly me out to Austin, Texas and put me up in a hotel room for the week that I wanted to stay. I told him I could stay a year because I had my B1/B2 US visa that I got when I was Superyachting. He asked how I'd survive with no money? I told him I could be a resident comedian at his new comedy club…Comedy Mothership!!! He laughed at me…then I said I'd suck his dick for it…he exploded laughing. Now these cunts of psychiatrists are giving me a depot injection that stops sexual arousal. You are not able to ejaculate and it is unusual to get a cunting hard on. JESOS the difference this time in!!! They are all being nice to me…all the nurses. Even a flirt from an ugly one. There is big changes happening.

RONAN THE NURSE MAN

Nurse Ronan from LK (Letterkenny) gave me good advice this morning. I was waiting on the Charity Housing first to bring me in my laptop but he suggested I start now with longhand. I shot him down because I prefer my laptop but then I thought about it and how fucking boring it is in here so I got some paper (discharge papers lol) and a black pen and started writing. It took me about an hour and a half to write the first chapter. I'm honouring Ronan (who has a wicked sense of humour) by calling this chapter Ronan the nurse man.

The shit with gaslighting has really calmed down in here. There is still one little head strong cunt...Mr. Witherspoon. He loves being in charge of me...I thought when I came in...let by gones be by gones so I offered my hand...he shook it sincerely then went into the bathroom and closed the window...as he was doing it he said...loud enough for me to hear..."Eyes like that I'll shake your hand!" He's a little Real I.R.A cunt. They fucking hate me. They've all been told to. It's about to stop completely BUT they are too late. I am still ending tourism. I've just heard through the nurses that I am getting...in their words...the jag. I made a joke with Ronan the nurse man about sucking my dick and now the little fucking LK tout fucking told on me!!!

I am thinking about all the friends that I grew up with. Damien Coleman was my best friend in school growing up…just as I transcribe this I heard one of the nurses say to the other keep that razor as a momento…I just had a shave and left the razor back to the female nurses lol…it's not the first time it's happened!!!…the nurse Eimear said "I'm going to!" and giggled…Damien was such a Badass!!! Connell was my friend outside of school but me and Damien…I call him Damo in iCon wildman101…always sat together for all those years. Sometimes the teacher would split us up then we'd make a deal with them and be allowed to sit together again. Just by accident after I got in some trouble carrying on in class, I discovered a lenient side to the teacher. She was so impressed with my work that she was even laughing at the boldness I got up to. It was a defining moment for me and changed my life. I figured as long as I was good at my work, people in authority would go easy on me for my misbehaviour. I still do this to this day. I act the bollocks but still get my work done to the best of my ability!!! Try it!!!!! As a Doctor once said to me after a Navy medical…"You've the heart of an Ox. A bollox!"

The Latvian asshole who is a patient here just reported me for being schizophrenic…imagine? The patients who are in the Real I.R.A are giving the nurses orders. I just listened to it down the fucking hall. He was talking then he dropped into the sentence "You're dead in the I.R.A". I fucking chewed his balls off.

I am listening to the biggest most conniving news station in the world. RTE…Radio Telefis Eireann. They are making up so much bullshit. They are all talking money now…ever since I got into Superyachting and brought the idea of that kind of wealth to the Island.

This little Island is the wealthiest Island in the world. The big pharmaceuticals made it that way. That is why the Real I.R.A do not want me to expose them. They are the dumbest fucking terrorists on the face of the Earth. They all want to be mentally ill. They hear from the other people who've been diagnosed that the doctors tell them they are extremely intelligent. The Real I.R.A all want that reputation. They say stupid things to me like "big pharma help people"…and the stupidest of all "Doctors care about people!"

Phew! No more gaslighting from the television!!! I turned it off…I am not schizophrenic…they are actually saying shit relative to me. I'm sure some of you must have noticed it on Irish television? It was all directed at me. I just had a burst of paranoia…AND ME THE FUCKING KING OF THE UNIVERSE!!! The paranoia was that the buck edjit psychiatrist would ask to see what I've written. The guy across the hall just said "He's a qualified writer…he's had his head down for the last few hours…he deserves respect around here".

The doctors everywhere are going to have a shit fit. I am destroying psychiatry!!! AND THEN…psychiatric nursing and psychologists. The only thing that will be used in relation to any of this other bullshit will be CBT…Cognitive Behavioural Therapy. The world will be completely saturated with highly paid well travelled counsellors. They will be young and old but they will be travelled extensively before they practice professionally. They will stay in hostels and get drunk and do drugs. They will be party animals because unless you have lived a life of extremes you cannot advise. The people that confide in Con are always the maddest and the baddest. These people would die for him. He has talked suicides down and stopped people really ruining their lives. The women that sleep with Con are his women for life. They will always fancy him. He is a Genius in bed. So attentive…so authentic. Con is Gods Gift that women dream of!!!

Talking about Gods Gifts…Ditsy Gilbert…Cons mate from London Town…who once asked Con was he in the I.R.A? They were driving 80 miles per hour along the highway in the South of France after doing a drug deal with the Russian Mafia…the Russian Mafia had the best Coke in the South of France…he was a contact of Ditsy's and Ditsy was feeding Con the Cocaine they had just procured as he sped along the highway when he suddenly asked him about the I.R.A. Con said no. He said ah come on you can tell me. Con thought nothing…not a fucking single thought of exposing himself to Ditsy, the biggest gossip in Superyachting history. Anyway, Adam aka Ditsy used to score with the most gorgeous women all the time. It was him that told Con about the screaming eagle. The screaming eagle is where you are shagging a girl on the beach missionary style. Then as you're pumping away…you pull out your cock…dip it in the sand and push it back in…the woman screams in agony lol.

Ditsy and me were like brothers. We had so much fun together. Cocaine, alcohol and chicks…Superyachtings the Mecca for it. A little asshole in Moville called Joshie thought he could use our family to get into Superyachting and piss his life away on drink and drugs and women… only if you're a mate you little cocksucker!!! He was overheard by one of my mates bragging in a pub…a pub I'm going to buy incidentally…that he was going into Superyachting to party like fuck…his exact words were "Drink, drugs and hookers!!!"…not a fucking chance would he survive and on top of that he would do what the other little cocksucker from Moville did…Lucas McStout aka McGuinness…another idiot I let in…just because he was friends with my younger brother…piss it away and not keep up appearances…they are not military standard like my family and the normal run of the mill in Superyachting…very high standard of people…Joshua still went to sea because my father was banging his mother after leaving my mother…in a blaze of Glory… mum pulled a shotgun on him SOS lol hahaha. She was full of drink on red wine. Dad grabbed the loaded shotgun and coward in fear of what could have happened. He got gun cabinets after that. I was so proud of mammy…anyway Joshie the little gobsheen is now working for the worst company in the world…in my opinion…I've heard stories. He fucking hates his life and has now got a child as well…what a fucking tosspot? Stuck in a loveless relationship because he did not pull out or did not have the savvy to fuck her off afterwards. I messaged him recently and offered him a chance for a job on a Superyacht because I felt like my da had made us brothers. He fucking wound me up...he said "We're not brothers!!!" I thought fuck you, you little cocksucker and wound the shit out of him and wait until you hear his response..."I hope you drowned..." he said. This fucking retard can't even speak English!!! I said to him "The word is not 'drowned' it's 'drown'!!!" You are a fucking waste of space. My da was just after a blowjob.

The man across the hall who is an undercover Guard...he's already blown his cover said "Man's writing a book and putting in jokes...and Bill McCann was gonna make him a pilot on the foyle." I was laughing at what I had written and he overheard me. Fucking idiot. I'm gonna NLP him so he'll never forget me. I'm adept at it. Get inside your head and jump around...

Just did it...I screamed loudly "GUARDS SUCK COCK...AFTER I STICK IT UP THEIR ASS!!!". Lol this is so much fun...my wife Gotta said to me that this time would be special and she is right so far.

Right ok time for a rest for a while. I'll be getting meds soons and I'm a little bored...not a fucking chance!!! See you soon lover boys and girls.

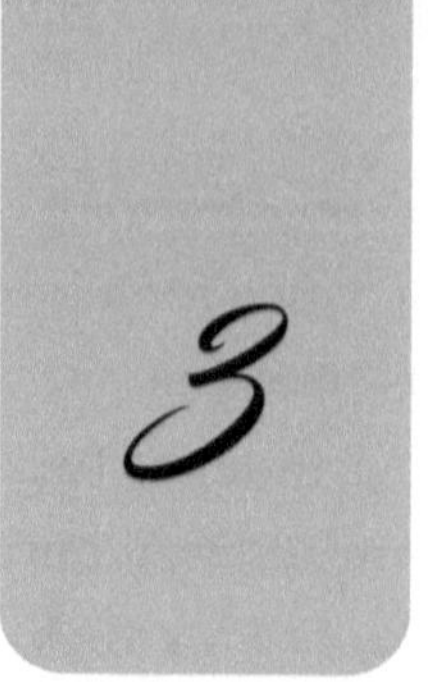

MIDNIGHT SUN

U s aliens have woken Con up to begin writing again…it's 4 O'Clock in the morning y'all!!!

The first thing on the agenda is the African nations. Con asked us a question. The question was "Do all black people come from the planet Negro?" That is what we told him. The truth is that all the different tribes of Africans come from different planets. Hence all the animosity and different dialects.

Cons friend Janie from down the country somewhere is one of the brightest girls Con has ever encountered BUT now he has encountered Gotta…outclassed! She even remembered being born. He is only just finding this out now but Janie is his little sister!!! Incest is best Con. They got it on. Lol. They were smooching for nearly 2 months. In between him riding other women lol. He fucked an Air Stewardess as well.

Trinity College is the most prestigious College in Ireland. Con is going to be an honorary English student there. He will receive an honor from them.

Con is also an Engineer. He will also receive an honour from DIT. Dublin Institute of Technology. He is wondering what the honour will be for? It will be for inventions. Con is going to solve Cold Fusion. We are going to tell him how to do it. You would not believe the brain on Con.

Tracy Cavanagh is a tramp lol...She loves Con. He would love to give her a baby. All of Tracy's brothers and sisters will help her bring up the most beautiful little girl. She will not have weight problems like her mother. Con can't wait to get into bed with her again and show her what he can really do. Tracys mother has a real shine to Con. She wanted them to get married. Con used to fantasise about fucking Tracys mother doggy style. He knows she is nasty. A good kind of nasty. A God fearing nasty lol.

Cons cousin Niall McCormick fucking hates the ground Con walks on. It doesn't even bother him anymore. As Snoop Dogg "Haters be hating...". The reason he hates him is because he believes he was born with a silver spoon in his mouth. Now that really fucks Con off!!!

Niall was the man who was spoiled. His mother done everything for him. Still fucking does. Con just felt a pang of guilt for telling these truths. Now he feels better when we say they are truths! Johnny Red, Styleys brother is a nasty piece of work sometimes. Just got to break into another story here. My surrogate Grandparents are coming through very strong from the ether. They are from England. My new country of origin. They are telling me that I should not...they repeat not...give my cousins a hard time. They say that people are only looking out for me. There is an element of truth in that but when Niall screams at you "TAKE YOUR FUCKING MEDICATION!!!" you must retire to the belief he is so closed to everything that is beyond his capability of comprehension. My surrogate Grandfather George Christopher Bennet just said "that sounds pretty good!!!" Now he says "Fuck him!!!". Lol. He always was a straight talker. They both agreed I was a Genius years ago. Anyway, Johnny Red was always back biting me. He used to tell Jim Farren on me. Jim was the self-proclaimed boss of Greencastle. I used to laugh like fuck. He had not got a clue how to run a crew. Now that's a line from a poem…here's a little poem about Jim Farren.

Clueless Jim Farren

The man is a blimp,
You'd swear he had a limp,
He walks like a gomey,
And tries to live like a stoney grey soil,
He thinks he's an intellectual,
Oh my God,
He was useless in school,
His older sister Cathy is a bitch,
Daddy knocked fuck out of her in front of me,
She hit me a slap,
When she was babysitting me,
I was so proud of daddy sticking up for me,
He threw her on the bed,
And started smacking her legs,
She was crying and whaling,
I was enjoying it,
I was only 3 or something,
I remember meeting Jim,
In his American Football top,
He was a bit weird…
Even at school,
He wouldn't be part of my gang,
He couldn't play football,
I haven't a clue what his memories,
Of school are…must ask him…we're still friends,
But he does not know,

How to blow,

A haystack down,

He hasn't a clue how to run a crew!!!

Johnny Red was actually really good to me. He was like a younger brother. We smoked copious amounts of Hash together.

Niall Hodd aka Doherty is my protégé. I told him how to get out from under his fathers clutches. His father I know for a fact does not know how much I influenced Niall Hodd. I was playing football in the back garden with my little bro Jailbird James. Niall came along in his tractor...man did he work hard...I walked up to him when he stopped to say hallo. I jumped up on the link box and began talking to him through the back window. It was a big fuck off tractor. They were rich. I asked Niall was he happy? I knew he wasn't. He was only in his early twenties and his whole fucking life was to be spent sitting in that tractor. I said to him after a brainwave...you should go to sea Niall. He said I can't...I've the farm to run. I said you can do both. He asked me how? I really love Niall. He is like a younger brother to me. My little brother Jailbird James thinks he is gonna keep a grudge going the rest of his life against my Pachsion brother Niall. I'll explain more later. James lost his job on the River Foyle because Niall took over the Pilots. I'll explain everything later on. Anywho, Niall asked me how he could do both? I saw him hooked immediately. His father really had no aspirations for him. I knew he was a bright lad and a party animal. I knew he'd have great fun. I told him get a job like me... month away and a month at home. I told him the blueprint of how to get it done...I'm such a Genius lol. He listened and said "Fuck it...I'm doing it". I said fucking right Niall I know you like farming but fuck you don't want to end up suicidal. He was totally and utterly in. Now he's a Pilot on the Foyle...so fucking proud of him and man did he have some adventures too!!!

This manuscript is being donated to the Sea Scouts of Ireland. It will bring them millions. I'm going to be their Patron. It's making me cry as I write this…fuck did I love my father and his take no shit attitude.

The Blackrock Sea Scouts were even following me on Facebook. I will visit them and find out what they need?

13 is my favourite number after 6. I used to count to 6 all the time when I was younger. I used to have OCD…Obsessive compulsive disorder. It was funny when I got older thinking back. Light switch things like that …all had to be done 6 times.

13 is a poignant number to me now. Daddy left me 13 grand in his will. I wondered did he do it as a joke? The reason I say this is because 13 in bingo is lucky for some! Daddy used to say it all the time. 13…lucky for some. Lucky I got some inheritance at all lol. He was a devious cunt as well. Not to be trifled with, he was a Genius. He'd fucking blow you away!!!

4

THE PROTAGONIST

Jim Farren wishes he was the Protagonist. He would love if my story was his. He has such an ego on him. He would not even let me have as drink in his house after a night on the beer with him. So fucking controlling.

We had a Pantomime in Shroove. It was a reunion for all those who performed in the Pantomime 30 years before. Mick Bennet aka Winifred…or little Red riding hood as the Ace Pilot in the Battle of Britain used to call her…she was his Engineer on his aeroplane… and she wore red overalls…he was called Douglas Bader and he was a real fucking Badass. Winifred gave me the book of his life when I was going off to join the Air Corps of Ireland. It didn't pan out for me. I'll tell you more later…Douglas Bader inspired the shit out of me. He inspired me to get up and get on with it. Mick was in the Wrens. The female wing of the Airforce of Britain…the RAF. Her and her husband George met and married in 6 weeks during the 2nd world war. Then they spent a year apart. George was in the Royal Navy. When the war was over, they reunited and opened a Supermarket in Blackpool, England. Then retired wealthy people to Ireland and opened up a pub and named it after me lol just kidding…they called it The Drunken

Duck. It became so famous. Every time my father was in, he'd joke with George "When you retire…I'm gonna buy this place off you!!!" Daddy was always drunk when he done this. George used to laugh at him but when it came time…George sold it to Daddy and we became child slaves. The Pantomime had all the original people and Mick wrote the script…she was so smart!!! She put in a Prince Charming. She wanted me to play Prince Charming. I was so in love with one of Jim's friends…Jamima…if you've read iCon wildman101…you'll remember her…the woman I done Shannon Airport for…she used to be one of my friends too but we drifted apart…that I tried buttering Jim up and asked him to play Prince Charming in the play so I could get with her. I don't know but I'm guessing that Mick was very disappointed. She just said to me in my head that she did not care as long as we all had fun. Daddy was even in it…he always wanted to be a Hollywood action Hero…I'll live his dream for him. Mick wrote me another part. It was Del Boy from the British television programme 'Only Fools and Horses' favourite catch phrase…Mick just interjected…so did George…Mick said "Jim couldn't act worth a fuck…pure arrogance made him do that!!!" George said that little hug I gave him when he was in Letterkenny hospital dying of Leukemia…he just said I felt like his son…I don't know what I thought of him…maybe a brother…he just saluted me and wiped a tear from his eye…I can see all of this in my mind. Mick just said make up with Brett Smith and that he is my older brother in Shroove and THAT is why nobody touched me at school BECAUSE if they did him and my cousin John McCann would kick the bejesus out of the them….now continue she said…I said consider it done…I've always loved Brett and JOHN MCCANN TOO. The line from Only Fools and Horses is "This time next year…we'll all be millionaires!!!" I was told I pulled it off. I love acting. I do it all the time in Real life. Jims performance was lack lustre. No real heart in it. He's not even from Shroove.

ALIENS

The aliens are so bloody pleased with Cons life on earth. He has achieved everything that we set out for him to do. He is the most underrated Hero on the planet. Joe Rogan is going to make him a Superstar. He loves comedy and telling stories. His humour has helped him survive through the most treacherous of lives. He is the ultimate comedian…he gets his humour from us. We tell him what to say.

Joe Rogan is Cons favourite celebrity in America at the moment. Joe came from nothing and made it big. His life is really interesting. Con will not be asking him about it on screen but they will burn the midnight oil after the show…Con will find out lots about him. Joe wanted to know about Dark matter and Con told him it was an invention just like psychiatry. Joe laughed at it. They have a great connection…we are going to tell you something full on…Joe is Cons older brother from Pachsion. So is Elon musk…high achieving family, eh?

The aliens Pachsion are about to leave Pachsion. There are thousands of Spaceships coming to earth. They will get here on the 4th of July. We told Con they were coming on the 11th of April but we decided that this book will need to be on the market before we get there. The aliens are all excited about meeting their King on earth. They know he's a Wildman and a complete fucking lunatic!!!

Con is not one bit disappointed about us not coming on his birthday. Something else magical is happening on that day. Con is getting laid. Mairead Butler…one of Cons women is going to suck his cock without a condom and Con is going to French kiss her with his cum in her mouth…he's never done a snowball before!!!

Cons favourite pub in Letterkenny is Sonny McSwines…it's so seedy. It reminds him of all the old sailor haunts around the world. He's been in lots of them. The psychiatric nurses are bitching in the other room. One little cunt said "You're not getting out the main door with that book!!!" And nurse Paula said she loves me…I mean really loves me… she told me…she is fucking smoking hot…"Just fucking watch me he's thinking" she said. Paula then said "They're thinking of putting a plaque up on the wall at the door…saying Con wrote his book here!" Paula's very temperamental. Just like all women. She just said "I'm out"…it's I.R.A speak…one minute they're "in" and next minute they're "out"!

The aliens are delighted Con sees the bigger picture. We are making America come alive. We will tell them to throw away all their psychiatric medication. They will listen. Another asshole psychiatric nurse just said and I quote him "You're not getting out of here with that book!!!"… they are bullying me again. They took my phone off me because I was reporting to the public on Facebook what way they were abusing me. Those fucking nurses are dead in the water.

They just said that I am writing on hospital property (Predicted date of discharge (PDD) papers lol) so they own my book!!! Lol fucking halfwits!!! It is fucking laughable…they can have it…I'll sit and write it again. Enda the skunknurse…sounds like poisonous weed…I shook his hand yesterday morning and gave him a terminal illness…now that's funny!!!...is behind it. He said they contacted the C.I.A and they told them to do it AND on top of that Siobhan Collins...my shrink... contacted Hereford...the SAS Headquarters. She got nothing out of them. That is the funniest thing I have ever heard. She wanted to find out if indeed I was in the SAS? I told them I was connected and I am. They are my third cousin lol.

Joe Rogan is doing his homework on me as well. He wanted me to be part of some fucking blockchain or other. I am fucking skint. I told him when I had money I would invest but I don't think he wants that!...He wants to make me a millionaire himself. Elon Musk is behind it...one of the Spirits that talk to me just said "He'll not IN control our Frodo!" lol I can't even remember what character Frodo is?

The psychiatric nursing is the handiest job in the world. At night they sit in comfy chairs reading books and fucking about on the internet. There comes Enda...laying down the law...telling everyone we do not want a book...it's all down to his mother he said...it's nuance for him she said to complain about the cold!!! That's why my mother put me in here...Enda just said he should have been in Austin in a hotel. Awww Enda sticking up for me!!!

Paula is making me coffee AGAIN!!! LOL she has the serious hots for me and I look like...well Mick just said I'd have rode every one of her Wren counterparts...fuckin' hell what fun that would have been? Mick just told me to wank over her in the shower this morning. I tried but I could hardly get it up with the fucking medication in me. JESOS is this stuff fucking poison?!!!

I'm fucking starving...breakfast is coming soon...I'll go for another smoke!!!

Fuck does Paula fancy me? Those fucking eyes lol just like the Stewardesses on the Superyachts. Fucking hell...every one of them flirted with me bar none…even some of the owners wives and daughters SOS lol!!!

Us aliens are itching to tell Con something that will blow his mind. Like we still have Dinosaurs. We do as well on special islands. They are confined by forcefields. They are our biggest tourist attraction. The people are protected by personal forcefields so they can walk about. The forcefield deters Dinosaurs from eating them. Still a bit risky I'm sure you're saying but we are so bloody advanced you would not believe. There are tags on the Dinosaurs…all of them…Con just asked are there Pterodactyls?...of course there are. It is amazing…we've done it. Made Con smile with excitement. He is gonna see it with his own eyes.

LUKE SKYWALKER

How did Luke Skywalker know what he got from Dada Con for Christmas? He felt his presents.

The Star wars movies are a premonition of Gene Wilder lol Gene Roddenberry about us coming. Our history is intertwined in the movies. Con is Luke Skywalker. You Americans are going to love this chapter. We know its gonna be your favourite. God does not exist. We are the only givers of life on the plane of Exorcith…that is where all life comes from. The aliens all over the universe are under our command. There is no other people in the universe other than those represented on earth in each of their relative countries.

Darth Vader is a true life character. There was a Death Star. We fought for millions of years against him. We were victorious. When we beat him…we were so happy. We wanted to see the reaction on earth of our history. It happened about a million years ago. Now it's over. Con won it for us then…he fought Darth Vader on a plinth with no special effects. They came to a gentlemans agreement that they would fight one on one. Con won. He chopped Darths head off. It was a bloody battle. They fought with knives!!! Con kicked his head off the plinth after he chopped it off…there was blood everywhere…and thus ended the war of the Universe. Then Con had a breather of a thousand years. Him and Gotta had sex 3 times a day for 1 thousand years…a bit like him and Fanjita…he is only finding this out now but she is also a sister…a fucking horniest in the universe sister…he will fuck her senseless again…SOON!!!

Darth Vader was his actual name. He came from Britannia. Britannia is the most volatile planet in the universe. They have so many wars going on. People are taken there from other planets to fight in their wars. They are mostly from the planet Negro. All the Darkies. The worst thing is the Negro people are so subservient that they think they chosen by God. We had to step in on their world. We had to stop the atrocities that were occurring every night and day. The war was so fucking terrible. It is the worst thing ever in the universe. We will tell you more throughout the book!!! Must go chop somebody's head off…he just came into my study and threatened me…that's what I call the sitting room here in this little buttfuck mental asylum lol… right here's me chopping his head off…"IF THE HEAD OF THE REAL I.R.A WANTS TO FIGHT ME HIMSELF…I'LL CHOP HIS MOTHERFUCKING HEAD OFF!!!"…that bloody silenced him. I just fucking screamed it lol…another one bites the dust!!!

PREDISPOSED TO DEATH

The Real I.R.A have plans to knock me down with their cars while I'm walking along the side of the road. The threat just came from across the hallway. He is in the Real I.R.A. There is also a dweeb of a man of Indian descent…them fuckers are only dangerous with a gun. Maybe a knife too if they get you from behind.

This will not ever take place. We are watching you…the human race. And listening to every thought you have. If Con is in any danger, we tell him. You will never hurt him. He is invincible. He is the KING OF THE UNIVERSE!!!

The Real I.R.A are the most manipulative, ignorant, belligerent, obnoxious, evil, sadistic…people who are predisposed to death…fear nothing people. They are all going to die of Cancer. The Cancer will affect them periodically all over the world so as not have congestion. It will be staggered over the next 3 years BUT trust me…they are fucking dead for what they have done to their King!!!

The other thing the Real I.R.A are going to be disposed of is their military intelligence…they have none. How do they EVER believe they are the rulers of the world? Brittania doesn't rule…no-one rules it apart from us.

Dublin City is my bloody home in Ireland. I love that little city. So fucking much history. I met my cousin Zabrina Shortt inside the G.P.O…the main Post Office in Dublin…that people, is where the 1916 Easter Uprising was held. You can still see the bullet holes on the walls on the front of the building. Zabrina arranged to meet her there. We met and I was in love all over again. Zabrina is my sister from Pachsion as well. We fucked a few times when we were young but Lord Jesus did she look hot when we met in the G.P.O. Our eyes locked and she smiled. I'm smiling writing this because it was so sexually charged. We done the French greeting…a kiss on the cheek. I wanted to lay her on the ground and ride the fuck out of her. She was one of my fantasy fucks when I was a teenager at Carndonagh Community School. I realised my dream at 17. We had just had our Debs or Formal and Zabrina came back with us to our tent. It was on full of beer and it was on our land right beside Cons Port…our little beach. I shagged her for a few minutes then asked her for a blowjob…"Ugh!!!" she said…"no way it's disgusting…too many germs!!!" lol I carried on fucking her. I did not even have a condom on. I pulled her down towards me. She was straddling me…and as I did…there was William Norris resting on his elbow and lying on his side at the back of the big Scout tent watching the whole thing. I gave him a wave and he smiled that big wicked grin of his…he's another brother from Pachsion, we are like twins. We are so close in age. Zabrina denies this ever happened now because she is the most prestigious of all Scientologists in the country of Ireland. I know she still fancies me. I can see it in her eyes and her body language when we are together. Her crazy brother knows about us…he is also my brother from Pachsion. Check him out on Google. Kristian Capulet Shortt. He's a born survivor. He was stabbed 17 times with a pair of scissors…he's a cut above. And of course, he survived. He's a Killer as well…and a loud mouth poet. He's got some great music videos…check him out on YouTube…buy his albums…and fuck does he have a serious temper. I was slagging him off about his life and daughter and he went clean fucking bananas. He is living in the Seychelles in Africa...near fucking Somalia the idiot lol trust him to live on the edge. He loves it there. He married a black woman...she is really dark and so exotic... she is so black she is nearly blue lol I made that joke up after reading Wilbur Smiths books. Check them out also...

Frank Shortt...Zabrina and Kristians father was arrested for having drugs on his property. He owned the coolest nightclub in Donegal, if not the country! That is where Kristian gets his ego from. Franks autobiography – Abuse of power, is a real good read. I read it in a day or two...his wife gave me a signed copy of it. Look it up online...Kristian needs the royalties from it lol.

It's my sister's birthday today. The 16th of January...the same anniversary of me getting stabbed in the head. Those I.R.A cunts came down from Belfast and stabbed me in the head because I did not phone my sister and wish her a happy birthday. Lol that's what I used to think when I was drunk sometimes. And guess who I thought was responsible?!!! My fucking Daddy!!! It was total bullshit but something like he would do!!! He was the Mafia Don in our country. Lots of people knew him as it but he kept a relatively low profile in crime.

He was in the Real I.R.A...he told me so. I was out on my own. I was the only person with an I.R.A background that would not support them. I was holed up in a hostel in Palma, Mallorca drinking like fuck when a vision appeared in front of me. You're not gonna believe who it was...? Queen Victoria of Britain. She told me "Take down the Real I.R.A!!!" I listened to her reasons and they all made very good sense... even as an Irish man and an I.R.A man. I was also signed up to the firm. I'm a K agent. Read Andy McNabb. Read all of them. Start with Bravo Two Zero. My cousin Moggy told me this. He was in the Parachute regiment in the British Army. I was so proud of him when he joined. He asked me did I want to join with him but I declined. He laughed at me and said "Too I.R.A?". I did regret it for a while. I really wanted to join the SAS. It looked so exciting. I've always wanted to be a Spy. It turns out I already was one. I just didn't know. My father was a Spy and he trained me but the training is so subtle that you have to figure it out for yourself. The moment I realised I was an I.R.A assassin was such a defining moment in my life. My father gave me 3 books to read. The first one was called Jig and the second one was called Jigsaw…can't remember the third but the first one was my favourite of all time I.R.A books. I did not know but they were I.R.A reading material. They are designed to tune your mind into the mindset it takes to endure intense situations such as interrogation and physical endurance. They help you to overcome the guilt of killing someone…not that I ever had a problem with that. I am the most cruellest of people when I want to be. I would kill men, women and children…no jesting…it is war… You feel a change in you after reading them. Both the Andy McNabb and the I.R.A books.

My cousin Moggy is about the hardest motherfucker I know. His nickname in the British Army was Arnie. They likened him to Arnold Schwarzenegger…his neck is thick as fuck from training. He used to do the Mike Tyson neck rolls all the time. And man does he have a wicked sense of humour. I want him to be able to come to Ireland on holiday. He hasn't been home since he joined the British Army. I know it hurts him but as his father Charlie said "There's still a few psychos about". I wanted to tell him that I was the Boss man and that Moggy would be fine but I couldn't guarantee it. There would always be some cunt that would attempt his life. Fucking cunts!!!

RAINBOW KISS

I want to address something very important here. It involves blowjobs…women should not…I repeat venomously…NOT make their men shower every time before a blowjob. Just fucking go with it. Don't worry if it's not that clean. Your juices in your mouth will clean it in seconds. And do not worry about a little urine getting in your mouth…swallow that baby.

As for Vaginas…make sure they're clean for they do smell.

All men should do this to their women. They should lick them out when they're on their period. The blood is not that bad a taste and oh my God will you make your women feel special and clean and so in love with you. That is called a Rainbow kiss.

My book iCon wildman101 is kind of a funny title. The iCon bit is obvious but not everybody knows what a wildman101 is. A wildman101 is where you French kiss the cum out of an asshole.

Blowjobs…they are the most supreme of ejaculations for a man. A woman must enjoy cunnilingus when the man knows how to do it properly. The best method of licking a woman out was taught to me by my sister from Pachsion…I did not know she was my sister…I still masturbate over her…the sexual urge that comes over me when I think of her is overwhelming. I fucking explode…apart from when I'm on this fucking depot injection. They just gave it to me last night. No more ejaculation for me for a month. I am so fucked off!!!

The way to give a woman the best orgasm of her life is to start with them lying naked on the bed…make sure the fucking room is warm… but not a necessity…beach or mountain top and kiss her lips, then neck, slowly running your tongue down to her nipples. She will favour one nipple in particular…especially if she has breast fed. Kiss around the sides of her breasts then trace your tongue down to her belly button. Play with it a while…DO NOT TOUCH HER PUSSY AT ALL until…then start with her knees…I know man it's a bit of a work up lol…run your tongue along the inside of her thighs…from her knee to her pussy…remember not to touch the pussy!!! Do this on both sides. She will be dripping wet by this stage. Then lick her pussy. Then open her pussy lips…let her guide you as well…don't spend too long on any of these moves…and put your tongue deep inside her. Use both hands and gently pull her pussy lips apart. Search for her clitoris with your tongue. It's at the top of her pussy. When you feel it, give it a suck. Then, with your tongue again feel the groove on it…in the middle. It is like a little bean…hence the phrase "Flicking the bean"…T-Dogs favourite saying…my other sister from Pachsion who I fucked as well. Once you establish the groove on the clitoris gently flick it over and back with your tongue. Rub her breast. Pinching her nipples. Not too hard… they are sensitive. Keep this up until she moans with pleasure when she starts cuming. She will go berserk for your cock…tell her "wait until you cum"…she will argue and tell you to put it in right away… you must be firm with her and tell her "I'm not putting it in until I can taste the juices in my mouth from your orgasm". They will concede. Then tell them they will have multiple orgasms if they wait until they orgasm before you put your cock in. When she eventually cums…do not be put off by any woman saying "I never had an orgasm like this"…

just tell them…"You've never had me before…" This may take up to half an hour on the first time. Women get very self-conscious about this kind of sex. They are so used to the social construct of letting the man just orgasm and that is it. Persevere men…do not let her make you give up because she loves you so much and can't stand to see you fail!!! I am changing sex for everybody. This will become part of your sex life every time you have sex. It will no longer just last a couple of minutes. And women if your man is drunk and wants a quick fuck… tell him to look into your eyes and masturbate. That will get them over it. Because you do not want to feel like some blow up doll. Help him with the masturbation. Maybe suck him off. When you give your woman the orgasm of a lifetime…lie on your left side if you are right handed…right side if you're left handed…take note little brother lol… lie her on her back…then put her right leg on top of your two legs… wrap your two legs around her left leg…I got a hooker off doing this… and penetrate her pussy with your cock. Use her left leg as purchase and pump her slowly…caress her pussy…tell her to masturbate herself as well…she can rub her clitoris…this sex position is a Position from the God…Constantine O'Donnell. It is Cons favourite position and you will achieve multiple orgasms for the women. Do not cum until she has nearly passed out with pleasure. This actually happens. They orgasm so many times that they feel faint. That's when you come dudes…ramp up the speed and hold on tight to her left leg and fuck her brains out. She will not be able to stop the screaming of pleasure!!! Go in peace to love and serve the Aliens!

PAULA THE NURSE

S he has got to be the coolest chick I've met in 20 years of my being in mental asylums. She is drop dead gorgeous and so bloody sound. I fancy the pants of her…and what a fucking ass on her!!!

I would like to give her a baby and 10 million euro to look after it. The child would be so intelligent and what a fucking voice it would have! She reminds me of…I think this is her right name…Mariella Frostrop…she had the sexiest voice on TV when I was growing up. Paula reminds me of her. She has such expressive eyes as well. Paula told me she loved me under her breath so no-one else could hear her. I was so overwhelmed that I did not take her on…but I've made sure she knows I fancy her as well!!!

NEW JOKES I'VE LEARNED

What did the mental patient do when the other mental patient asked for an orgasm? He done it remotely…true story…it was me giving the orgasm…she walked around in a daze for the next 2 days glowing and hardly talking lol.

What did Doctor Collins aka Siobhan do when I came on her face?…she said you are sexually overt.

How does Dr. Cliff Haley propose to his wife all the time when they fight about him only cuming every few years?…he drops to his knees and pulls her Vagina lips apart and yells "Con are you in there?"…she orgasms every time.

Dr. O'Donnell…no bastarding relation…has such pudgy hands…what we're wondering is how long the fat cunt will take to decompose when Con puts a bullet in him?…just kidding…there will be no trace back to him BUT that fat cunt is dying!!! He is responsible for labelling Con paranoid schizophrenic. Dr. O'Donnell is Dr. Noir in iCon wildman101.

How many psychiatric nurses (excluding Paula & Gotta aka Sinead) does it to make a bed?…depends on how much spunk I've sprayed on it lol…true story!!! I was just admitted on New Years Eve 2020 and I nearly had a kiss on the lips from another hot nurse…a married one to boot…fuck does she fancy me…she was sat beside me and had this look on her face that said "Fuck it!!!" then she said "I'm naked…" we were on our own in the movie room here in letterfanny mental asylum…I thought about standing up and putting my erect cock into her mouth…she would have sucked me off…I knew by the look in her eye…Jesus Christ how many times have I masturbated over that… God bless you Emma. Andy Pandy's niece. C/O of Bloody Sunday for the I.R.A.

Fiona Noonan will probably die of embarrassment when I tell this joke…How many Fiona's does it take to counsel Con?...None. You fuckers just give him a blowjob like she did!!!

Ferg and Enda are the retards of Letterkenny mental asylum. One has Cerebral palsy and the other is terribly balsy…Enda told me the I.R.A would cut my hands off if I went to R.T.E about the abuse he was giving me!

MICHAEL THE NURSE

Michael the nurse used to be scary to me. Those fucking piercing eyes. Reminds me of the I.R.A man Martin McGuinness. He had the scariest eyes in history. Anywho, Michael is a bit of a mentor in the literary sense. He loves reading. He have me the biggest book about one family…The Kennedys. JFK and all that Jazz. It was really interesting. But now I've gone off him…he now has a vendetta against me. I told him some info about me…I told him about Drea. I told him I'm going to marry her. He is so fucked off. He is talking it over with Paula my favourite apart from Gotta aka Sinead…in their office…I can hear every bleeding word…but she is falling out of favour too. I asked her for some Gaviscon and milk and she said I'll get it in a minute. "I'll bring it to you" she said. She still hasn't appeared…Michael is now saying "I'm contacting the Bombardiers and telling them he is very dangerous!"…Andrea already knows that lol. All her boyfriends are dangerous. She is another sister from Pachsion…she is the most beautiful of my women apart from Gotta!!!

Right, back to the story…Our Con is a Genius. He has rocked and rolled the world…Michael is still talking about me…he just said "There is nothing we can do about him in Superyachting". I'm laughing my ass off lol…they are talking about me incessantly…Now Fiona Noonan is involved…she fucking hates me…hahaha…she would love to give me a blowjob again.

Michael just said "If he threatens the human race, they'll put a freeze on his books!!!"

I'm a hitman…I don't give a shit what he thinks.

PSYCHIATRY IS DEAD

Dr. O'Donnell has misplaced his jawbone calling me paranoid schizophrenic. He is in mortal danger from the Racons. The Racons if you remember are my army on earth to protect me and my siblings. They are all over this world. The fat fuck O'Donnell…fuck has he let the O'Donnell name down…is about to be thin for the first time in history of his time on earth. When he decomposes, he will be like a normal human being…nice and thin…I'll dig up his bones and present them to the President of Ireland…Conor McGregor. I will have them treated and make a skeleton of them and ask Conor McGregor if he would be so kind as to put it at the door of his new Presidential house to warn all the other psychiatrists what will happen them. The Michael cunt is after slagging me saying "if he was an 'A' student – you would hear the pages turning"…he is in for as nasty slagging this fucking minute…I'll even tell you what I am going to say to him…I'm going to ask him did he give me the Kennedy book as a warning? He will say what do you mean? Well the daughter of Joe Kennedy was given a lobotomy…let's see what he says…that was funny as fuck!!! He was stuck for words lol.

Anywho, psychiatry is dead!!! I'm killing it. I'm reading house…I'm getting rid of the cocksuckers. They are never ever ever practicing law again SOS lol medicine. They can go into construction the soft mother fucking cunts. Let them see how hard life actually is and we'll pump them full of psychiatric medication and see how they fair out climbing up high fucking buildings under construction…see if they have the balls for it?

Psychiatry as Tom Cruise says is a Pseudo Science. I support him 1 million per cent on this point but the rest of his religion is absolute bollocks…BE VERY CAREFUL WHAT YOU SAY ABOUT SCIENTOLOGY…Ooooo I'm so sacred Tom…what will happen me? Lol. The Real I.R.A joined Scientology after I went into them and done a 5 hour interview with them in the old church of scientology in Dublin. The Real I.R.A are the biggest bunch of tossers on the planet. They have full access to all the information scientology have on life…L.Ron Hubbard was a complete fucking idiot…Jesus Christ he even said to them "If you want to be a Billionaire…create your own religion!!!" It must have been fun for him to talk to people who were so susceptible to his bullshit talk about aliens…my very own cousin Kristian Capulet Shortt devoutly believes in him. I laugh my as off at what he has written. Kristian was all excited that I was reading what he recommended as introductory reading material to his life in scientology…the Real I.R.A are sitting at home scratching their big thick heads…Dennis McGonagle from national school in Greencastle came to mind when I wrote big thick head…he was such a dummy in national school…I once threw a compass at him, He was sitting opposite me being a bully in class. So, I picked up my compass and threw it like a throwing knife???!!! Kids do this when you're angry at a bully…it stuck into his stomach. I was so proud of myself…still am lol…the teacher went nuts…that big fat lazy stupid cunt…biggest boy in class…told the teacher…the teacher put it in my school report to my parents at the end of the year…my father was so proud of me lol he ate the bollocks off me…that big fucking dumbo Denis or big D as we used to call him when we liked him told my little brother on his wedding day that he was the main man on the playground at school when we were young...he said the teachers told him...and I do not doubt this...that he had to keep an eye on me...in other words tout on me...tout means to grass someone up in I.R.A speak...about what the fuck the scientologists are worshipping? They believe in aliens but we have never spoken to them. As Con said to Kristian that idiot L.Ron Hubbard was a fantasist and a fucking fiction writer...I told him it was gobbledegook...he went fucking mental...and said "Be very careful what you say about scientology..." Phahahahahahaha...then he blocked me again on WhatsApp lol for the Nth time hahahahahaha.

PRE-BREAKFAST

It's 08:07am and I am waiting on my breakfast…what a fucking plan!!! Gotta came up with it. The plan was to make myself so inept that they would think my mental health is deteriorating lol fuck that!!! I was having a whale of a time…throwing the rubbish at my feet all over the house…not washing my clothes and not shaving or cutting my hair…I shave it to the bone…my mother says whenever I do that…I look like a thug…I replied "Well if the shoe fits mammy!!!" She threw her eyes up to heaven.

Chloe the student nurse just came in to take my blood pressure. It's the most important job they have they have. They do it for 4 years. They walk around with the blood pressure machine like they are in charge of a Supertanker lol fucking assholes. I stripped off for Chloe…I took all my upper body clothes off…Chloe was affronted…she asked do you not have a T-Shirt? I said I do and pointed to the bundle of clothes… then I said it's in there…she continued and took my blood pressure… then I asked her did she like my tan?…she took a look without thinking and said yeah…I said I like your tan too. She said yeah ginger…I said the tan on your face and she did not even bloody say it was make- up… some of these women in Ireland do not have a clue of how to behave around a superior man. She tried being cheeky so I said the tan on your face doesn't match your arms. Then I said not unless you join all the freckles up. She walked off at that and I said BYE CHLOE sarcastically lol.

Anywho...as Styley would say...I've forgiven him for his disbelief of me...can't wait until I tell him everything about me...and him believe it...he has such a brain on him...if only he would use it...he'd be brilliant at computing...anyway back to Gottas plan...her plan was to act the mental patient until his mother saw how he was living and raised the alarm...Gotta knows the future...this has all been planned...a nice 5 star mental asylum to write the final book...we mean that...Con thought he'd be writing for the next 10 years...the fucking headache of it!!! Do not know how Stephen King does it...especially without drugs. Con will be writing a blog and everybody on the planet will subscribe. He will write 5 pages a month. It will detail his travels on his Superyacht all over the Globe. The aliens will be travelling with him. They will fly to the destination of Cons choice and have the whole planet watching on the internet as he approaches the desired berth of his bitches lol men of the cloth SOS there will be no more clergy or Rabbis or any other bible bashing cunts. The Special Forces of the world will make every country safe from terrorism...that includes the I.R.A SOS lol. I'm the Head of the I.R.A!!!

DR. MO

I got chatting to the doctor this morning. He was really sound…not poisoned yet by the fucking vile psychiatrists there are in this hospital. He was telling me that Libya was a dream to live in. Everything was free. Then he said I mean everything. He chose medicine as his career. He said it was like going to a buffet and just deciding what would I like to eat…looks like he ate quite a bit from his girth. I'm now listening to a phone conversation in the other room really loud so I can hear it. They are saying that they are going to make me permanent if I don't calm down…I'm about to scream…UP THE RA!!!

Dr. Mo is from Sudan…I asked him was he rich?…he laughed and said no way! I said you must have to become a doctor…then he said I grew up in Libya. He said he thought a loaf of bread was money when he lived in Sudan. He told me that Gaddafi supported the I.R.A. He said that Gaddafi supported over 200 militant organisations around the world. I did not know that. I said the RA probably got their guns for free and he laughed his head off…he wanted to be a militant himself!

POGO

I remember once I came back from sea…I was full of beans and full of life. I went out for the night in Moville on the screaming fucking piss. The people were loving me. All the women were all over me. This other arrogant asshole George McCormick…Styleys cousin… arrogance runs deep in that side of the family…anywho George was standing at the bar smoking. I knew he smoked Silk cut but I thought fuck it I'm gasping for a cigarette. So, I shouted to him…I seen him as one of the family because he was dating my older cousin Karen who incidentally is my sister from Pachsion…her and her other two sisters…I only fancy the youngest one…she's the little bad girl…anyway George fucking shouted at me…the place was packed and I was up on a stage type alcove with all the women and my mates…none of them had cigarettes…so anyway George shouts at me "Fuck off…buy your own cigarettes!!!"…then he fucking adds insult to injury and says in front of all my friends "Who do you think you are? You come back from sea and think you're the man!!!" I fucking was gonna knock him out….I knew I could kick his ass. That was it. I just left it. I carried on getting drunk. Then after the pub closed, I was standing beside the big tree in the square in Moville. I was standing on my own. George comes over with Mickey pogo. They were 7 or 8 years older than me. I was only

18 and pretty light. But I had a punch that would sink a battleship…
George comes over and says "You think you're tough?" I said what the
fuck do you mean? Then he said "You couldn't take me and Mickey
pogo"…I looked at pogo…and I remember the fat cunt slapping me on
the face before…I always wanted revenge for that…another story…I'll
tell you later…this is a big fucking book…300,000 words lol it could
be if I wanted to write it…I'll save it for the blog…as soon as I met
pogos eyes I could tell he would have beat me…as fucking if…I was
gonna rip his fucking eyes out. That's what you do with big men like
that!!! Mickey pogo looked at me and just looked menacing…I said to
the two of them "It takes two overgrown men to beat little old me?"
Mickey went nuts…about to thump me.

George put his finger up to my face…I said "Get your finger out of my
face before I break it!" George went fucking nuts as well. Mickey was
pogoing…bouncing up and dow. I said "Fuck away off and leave me
alone…I do not know what Karen sees in you, you arrogant cunt!!!" He
fucking went ballistic…the word ballistic reminds me of a punishment
essay I wrote in 3rd year at Secondary school…I was caught throwing an
eraser at one of the assholes in the class and the teacher got mad and
told me to write an essay on ballistic missiles as punishment…I had one
night to write it…I went home and opened up an encyclopedia…this
is the days before the internet…and found ballistic missiles and wrote
about them…he was well pleased but I did not like him much more
after that lol I lie he was my favourite English teacher. We were doing
honours English…he taught us loads of stuff…he's part responsible
for my writing…George lost the plot…I said "Go on hit me…see
what happens!!!" I looked around them to see who of my mates were
there…I saw a few of them and started laughing. They were two of
the hardest cunts I had in my team…I egged George on…he looked
around too and immediately backed down. He spotted them as well, I
guess. pogo was shitting himself…McCole was drunk…I dunno what
they were thinking but their arrogance definitely got the better of
them…George went to put his finger up again…I pushed it away…I

thought about smacking the cunt square in the nose and kicking pogo in the balls...George didn't get angry and said to me "I'll see you in the morning when you're sober..." I said "Whatever"...

The next morning I was still in bed when my wee brother came down to my bedroom and said to me "Con wake up...Con wake up would you?"...he was 8 years old...makes me angry even thinking this... then he said "George is in the Kitchen, he wants to speak to you..." I said "George who?" He said "George McCormick"...I said "What the fuck does he want?" "I dunno" he said. I put on a pair of jeans and walked up the hall. I was still drunk but it came flooding back to me...the nights events the previous night...I thought I'm gonna have some fun here. I walked into the Kitchen and there's George with a big angry head on him...I decided to fuck with his head and said "Yes George how's it going?" My little brother was watching...a brainwave came over me...I'll show little bro how to deal with threats from assholes...I was going to grab George by the throat (parents weren't there lol) and drag him out onto the grass and kick the living fuck out of him and say to my younger brother "DON'T LET ANYBODY EVER PUSH YOU AROUND!!!" but I didn't. I thought of my cousin Karen. I knew it was going to marriage. So, I decided to hear him out. He started spouting off telling me he would beat the hell out of me if I ever disrespected him like that again. I lost the plot...the kicking was coming...I only had my jeans on...I did not care...bare foot or not...I would have kicked him to pieces...no bloody way was he talking to me like that in front of my little brother. I said "George get the fuck out... you come to my house and threaten me on my own door step...get the fuck out before I kill you!!!" I looked over at my younger brother and winked...it didn't mean I wasn't going to do it lol...I was roaring it at him...I can be so fearsome when I want to be...he jumped in the car... it was brand new...as he was getting in I said "Like the new car...health to drive..." cool as you like. He fucking flipped. He took off spinning backwards...wheels screeching on the pavement...then he sped up the driveway and went screaming up the road…my little brother said "I hope he doesn't crash!!!" he was laughing his head off.

The aliens taught George McCormick a lesson. They gave him and my cousin Karen a retarded kid as a first born. My mother was drunk and said to my father "Do you think that handicapped child has anything to do with George falling out with Con?" She was deadly serious…we put the idea in her head…Con's father said "Don't even dare say that in public…of course it wasn't". It did not convince my mother…she's an alien too!!!

ALIENS REVENGE

Us aliens do not care for human life the way you humans do… hence all the suffering in the world. We designed the planet and we put every earthling on it. We are so vengeful of anybody that stands in Cons way…we are killing people that have well and truly fucked him up…Doctors, nurses, members of the public and Gardai Siochana. When Con was sectioned for the first time back in 2006… the arresting Guard who was bullying him was given Leukemia…he did not last long…let that be a lesson to the rest of you Guards…Don't fuck with him.

Con's father also fell victim to us. He was trying to control Cons life for the worse. He was fucking killing him. Not on our watch.

Cons Auntie Fay was not very nice to him when he was down playing at their house with his cousin Gemma. We gave her Cancer of the bowel. She died as well but she now appears to him looking to be fucked up the asshole…she fucking loves it when he orgasms…she can feel it. All spirits can feel orgasms…that twat Russell Brand said in his book My Booky wooky that an orgasm in French is called a 'petite mort' or little death because of the guilt you feel afterwards…the only reason people feel that when they are fucking is that not a nice spirit is inhabiting them. He needs exorcised…I'll suck him off…see how he feels then lol I'd blow his fucking mind!!!

Jim Farrens older brother Benny hung himself at age 18. He was drunk and angry at his mother…he was a bully. We told him to hang himself because we did not want Con under threat from Jim. Jim would've won the playground if Benny was alive. He once threatened Con with Benny…Con said "Fight me yourself…" Con never thought about threatening Benny with his father. He always fought his own battles.

Cons next door neighbour Martin Lynch is a fucking tool of a man. Con took a serious dislike to him when he told Con that he used to beat his wife all the time. Con was shocked at how open he was about it. Then came the clincher…he started laughing and said he smacked her one time on the mouth and there was blood pumping out of her… Con nearly knocked him out but got him back another way…we told you…we are very vengeful!!! He told him that his brother that was shot by the I.R.A during the troubles was shot because he was a tout. He lost the plot and tried hitting him with a poker. Con pretended he was afraid and said "Martin…Martin…think of your heart…" he knew that would wind him up even more!!! Martin put down the poker and screamed "Martin McGuinness came to our house after it and said it was an accident…he said they got the wrong man!" I said nothing and never darkened his door again.

Cons mother was also given Cancer. She was such a bitch to young Con. And fucking old Con too. We decided to lighten the load on the O'Donnell household…his father would've got a new woman in no time. The only reason we wanted his mother was for the professional athlete DNA. Her father played for Ireland at soccer…we wanted her temper as well in him…Gotta thinks this is hilarious…Con is thinking of all his mother's traits which he enjoys. Con thinks her intelligence as well but the intelligence came from his father's side. Cons father was so heartbroken when his mother contracted Cancer that we decided to let her live but gave her a fucking message...be fucking nice...she was given lymphademia. She was still a hateful cunt!!!

DADDY CON THE HERO

M y father was something special. He was so fucking cool growing up. I felt so protected everywhere I went with him. He was charismatic with everyone he talked to…it rubbed off on me. I worked alongside him as well in our family bar and restaurant. The pub was so much fun. I had so much women there. Blowjobs, full on sex…wait till you read my blog…I'll be putting in little anecdotes in it from the Drunken Duck days. My father said to me when we bought it "Nothing leaves this bar…whatever happens within these 4 walls…stays there". Total Mafia. Omerta, No tales out of school.

My favourite story about my Da was one of his car crashes…he had a few of them. It was early morning after a long night behind the bar. A few of the customers has stayed to the last…I just got a buzz out of reminiscing there…Harry Frizzell as usual was last to leave…one of Harry's jokes…he was a bit of a Comedian…"Why is your shit tapered? So your ass doesn't close with a bang! (then clap your hands a slap!!! and laugh lol…always laugh…you don't have to be dead pan all the time…but it is fun dead panning people lol pull the fuckin' piss out of those green to the world Millenials!!!)…Anywho Daddy left him home and on the way back crashed into…not to his dying day when asked...he said it was an accident and nobody believed him...he was in a feud with some out of towners and he crashed the car into their new fence and landed upside down in our brand new Mondeo. It was a flying machine. I'd already crashed it. We only had it 3 weeks...I was driving my sister up to get homework off one of her classmates...my nemesis Tom Harkin lol the Principal of the NATIONAL SCHOOL in Greencastle...anyway it was his daughter Aine...always got on with her and Fergal his son...he always had a glint in his eyes for me...I used to laugh...he knew I tortured his father lol...I was flying up the road and it was pissing down with rain...I was doing about 80mph when my sister got freaked..."Slow down" she said "You're gonna crash". I slowed down then came around a corner approaching the crossroads in Greencastle...right a Batty's shop...and as I did this imbecile was coming across the road to the shop on the other side. I wonder was it planned? Fucking assholes...we were always targets growing up...It was Sunday...my sister was cramming...She's very good at English... the asshole came straight out in front of us. Lucky that my Da had taught me very very well how to drive from an extremely young age...I think about 2 if I'm not mistaken. I clutched and braked and swerved out around him. There was a wall on the other side of the road with a raised garden behind it, so no give, if I had of hit it. As I swerved, I hit the front of his car. I skidded to a halt. Jumped out and was fit to be fucking tied I was so angry. I'd asked my father when he was teaching me to drive those roads who would be at fault if a car came out like that? He said they would. I knew I was in the right so I picked up his bumper and held it above my head and ran at his car about to smash his head in. The shop keeper Batty who was also a Guard came out and hollered "CON CALM DOWN!!!" He was An Gardai Siochana...same as me...the I.R.A police...Connells father. Remember him? Anyway it all calmed down and my Da and now nemesis of the O'Donnell family lol Bill McCann came to our aid. They looked at our car and decided there wasn't toO much damage...they definitely both had drink taken lol and they decided to just change the burst tire and complete the mission. Their reasoning was if we didn't do that, we might end up afraid to get behind the wheel again…I have to admit I was a bit shook but driving up to Harkins house with the steam flying out of the bonnet was hilarious. My sister Margaret was howling laughing too. She said they're not half fucking wise…back to the not near wise… my father ended up, upside down on the roof of the car with the til from the cash register in the car. He was so cool. He phoned us at the house. He knew we wouldn't be in bed yet. We'd be out in the garage playing pool on our pub pool table…man did that get some use…every house in the world should have one…he told us what happened and to phone Paddy Doherty's number to tow it away. We done it and phoned Paddy. Once that was done, we ran up the road to find where the car had hit. We were so excited. Well only excited because he was okay. I'm just thinking, he definitely done it on purpose lol bad motherfucker lol. As we were running up, we met him sauntering down with the til under his arm…it looked so fucking funny. He was so casual looking. MISSION COMPLETE probably lol. I asked him did he think we could flip it onto its wheels? He was definitely drunk…he said we can give it a go…we went up and it was so fucking funny. He had driven straight through their new fence at the road and landed in their street upside down. There was money everywhere…the phone was lying on the ground where he'd phoned from upside down inside the car. He phoned us straight after he crashed. When we decided we couldn't throw the car over…I thought we need some help! So, a brainwave came over me and I said to Daddy I'll get the Mulhalls up and maybe all of us could do it? Right he said go ahead. I went up to Mulhalls house which was opposite the crash site and was easy to get into. They always leave the back door open. I walked in quietly and up the stairs. I opened the boys bedroom door quietly…it was about 5 in the morning but it was summer time so it was bright daylight…I started hollering "DADDY'S CRASHED THE CAR!!! I said it 3 times…all 3 of them jumped up out of bed from a sound sleep…probably a drunken sleep and started asking was he okay? I broke my balls laughing and said he was fine. They said "You cunt!!!". They got dressed and came down to look at the car. Michael Mulhall...the eldest of the boys...a couple of years older than me...who incidentally bullied me when I was 4 years of age...I never forgot it...it was my first day at school and he came running over and scratched my face with his finger nails. I thought what a wee girl? He left me bleeding between the eyes...I had the scar for years. Everytime I looked in the mirror I thought of him...I got him back...I fucked his wife when they were broke up before they married...he never knew lol...

So, there we all were looking at the car and Michael said "We'll never throw that fucking car over!!! I'm going back to bed". So that was it. We went home down the road. The change was rattling in the til under my Da's arm. I asked him how come there was still change in the til? He said I picked up as much of it as I could...we all exploding laughing.

Another story that makes me laugh is when it was my 17th birthday and we were collecting firewood for the bonfire for the party. There was a dead tree in the field. The field was very flat and you could drive a car on it. We tried chopping the dead tree down but it was too dry. Our saws kept sticking and we had no oil for lubrication for the blades. My father said to us...me, Connell and Michael Mick...you'll meet Michael Mick later on in my life...saw the other side of the tree as much as you can. So, we did as he said. He took us to Derry the day before to get beer for the party. Connell and I spotted Carlsberg Special Brew at 9% alc. a can SOS lol...we bought a case of it. Neither of us had ever tried it. My Da was laughing at us. He knew we wouldn't be able to drink it. It is fucking disgusting. Anyway, we cut as deep into the trunk of the tree as we could and when we couldn't saw anymore Da pulled out a rope. He'd disappeared but came back. He did not say where he was going. He pulled it out as a surprise. Then he said "Right Con put them climbing skills to good use...up that tree as far as you can and tie this to it!" I laughed my head off and took the rope and climbed up the tree. It was dangerous. Branches kept breaking on me. I climbed up as far as I could and then tied it to a sturdy bit of the tree. I climbed back down and Da tied it to the toe hitch. He reversed to the tree, then drove up the field quickly. The tree bent over then pulled back up again, lifting Da's car off the ground and spinning it around. We all started laughing…this is great craic we thought!!! Da lost the plot…all we could hear was the fucking rev of the engine. Michael Mick said it first…he said "It's coming down now I guarantee you!!!" he was pissing himself laughing. Da reversed back to the bottom of the tree. Made sure the rope was free to extend, then got back in, revved it again…the fucking Dukes of Hazard…took off spinning…grass flying everywhere. The tree started bending and with the speed my Da was doing he would have brought down the Empire States building. The tree fell…we chopped it up and local youngsters helped us carry it over to the Big White Bay…the coolest beach on Earth…right beside the lighthouse in Shrove…where I had a joint at the top of one time…cheers Brett!

Later that night, my mum and dad came over to the party to see how things were going. We were all kind of drunk. There was about 50 of us…

To my friends of youth

We had a blast,
When I think of the past,
We had a youth,
That was rather uncouth,
We had so much fun,
Without the guns,
Skinny armwrestling,
And older women nestling,
Lying in their rugs,
Cos according to the psychiatrists,
Our mums didn't give us hugs!!

I was smoking a cigarette. My Da said "I didn't know you smoked?!" I said "Only when I'm drinking." He was actually proud of me. He smoked about 150 a day. People used to ask him if he smoked many? He'd reply "I eat them!!!". They'd always laugh.

This anecdote makes me so proud of my father. He settled a feud I was in. The local Hoodlums 'THE GREASERS of Moville'…Self Styled drug enforcement law. They used to beat up anyone in town that had anything to do with drugs. It was my 18th birthday and I decided to have a big bash for it. I wasn't expecting the bashing that happened. My cousin Danny McCann…the Ladies man…lol he is Bills older brother…gave me his PA system. A couple of speakers he used for his band. We had the pub at the time so I had plenty of contacts to help me have the bash of a lifetime. There was no food. Just drugs and alcohol. We held it in an old derelict school (my fathers old school when he was a youngman) right beside our pub The Drunken Duck. There was about 150 people at it. Everybody was getting nicely pissed. Then 'The Greasers' turned up. BOOM!!! A fight ensued. We are the Shroove ones…as my little sis says "IN SHROOVE THEY CAN'T HEAR YOU SCREAM!!!"…the outlyers. The ones with the guns. Up the RA!!!

John McCartney…a friend of the families…a bit more than a friend. He was like a big brother to me. He was a soldier in the Irish Army for years until he captured a terrorist then started drinking with him…got drunk and the guy escaped lol. He is a fun guy. Not to be messed with but these fucking greasers were tubes. They thought that they were invincible. What were they doing there? I had no ties with them at all. It was a showdown. My father's friends kicked their fucking asses. John went into Soldier mode and kicked the Christ out of a few of them. Charless Hegarty kicked one of them in the nuts. I watched him do it. The guy fell on the ground and started crying…tears running down his little footsoldier face. There was about 20 of them. They obviously like the odds lol idiots. The guy that was lying crying about his nuts was laughed at. Charless said "He'll know where his balls are in the morning!!!" Daddy said John McCartney was so drunk and in Killer Mode, he was holding him back but he was roving him around with him looking for a target…her picked one out and let him go…John ran in and demolished the guy. He was fucking insane that night. I missed it all. I was in the back of a car getting it on with Tina Urbas. A hot bit of stuff from Moville…McCourts (his mum is O'Donnell) ex!!! Well broke in lol. I was just fucking getting into her knickers when somebody came to the car and said Joe the Greaser wants to fight you! I jumped out and said "Where is the cocksucker?" We ran over and there was a stand off about 20 feet apart. The Greasers where on one side and all my friends and father's friends where on the other. We were all lined up. Then they backed down when they saw I was like John McCartney only sober. I was going straight for Ray. Joe's younger brother. I heard he was the psychotic one. I thought take him out of the picture first. Then I'll fight Joe. They could tell by me that they were going to die. They headed for the hills. They ran like fuck…lucky cos no-one would hear them SCREAM!!! Phahahahaha. The whole lot of them ran like the gutter rats they are. Scurrying up the road.

My friend Damien Coleman had two black eyes…my father said there wasn't a man in Greencastle the next day that did not have a black eye!!! Damien was asked the next day by some girl what happened your eyes? His reply was "DEA!!!"

ZION

....

H AIL HITLER!!! No Jew alive likes to hear that! I don't really give a shit. They are the virus of the universe. They were not given a country on earth because they would be the most vile people on the planet if they were all together. They will be given one now that their plan for world domination has been thwarted by none other than King Constantine.

The Jewish people have some redeeming qualities. They care about… SOS no they fucking don't. They are money grabbing cunts. They are so tight fisted…Put a lump of coal in a Jews hand and tell him to squeeze his fist…Come back in a week and you'll have a diamond. That's how tight fisted they are.

The Jewish people invented psychiatry. Sigmond Freud was the forerunner in all this psychoanalysis bullshit. Figuring out the human brain. As if they can look inside your mind and figure out all the emotions of every individual…we are the only people that can do that. They are lucky they are not being exterminated. Con has beaten them at their own game. He has taken them down off their high life loving oh wait…that's Con…he has taken them down from the Egocentric twisted mindboggling fucking perch of Superiority over everybody that aren't Jewish. They have such a feeling of inferiority that is masked with so much reliance on their intelligence.

Hitler was one of our men…he is a brother of Con's. Con just felt a bit of pride. He always admired Hitler. He felt bad for the Jews until that man Con came into contact with their beliefs on mental illness. Everybody that works for the mental health services worldwide is brainwashed into believing that Jews are correct.

The mental health services are corrupt all over the world. They manipulate people who are so vulnerable…that was my inspiration to help them…the patients…not the effing jews…lol. They had nobody to protect them. I knew I could withstand the bullying and coercion. They cannot beat a killer of my stature. I am an I.R.A Assassin.

The I.R.A are being drawn into my war with the pharmaceuticals kicking and screaming. They do not want to ruffle feathers with them. The big pharmaceuticals have made Ireland the richest country in the world. The I.R.A are receiving money from them to protect them. They use the money for drugs and arms (Guns & Bombs…sounds like a rebel band name).

The Jewish people feel at ease in the I.R.A's company…not for fucking long. I'm in charge now. I am not one bit afraid of them. They lock me up all the time and I just take the cunt out of them morning, noon and night.

The people that are going to suffer the most when I am in charge of everything on this planet are the Jewish people. THEY WILL KNOW PERSECUTION…THEY CRUCIFIED MY BROTHER JESUS…I am the Second cominG!!!

ORIANA

At last I met a stunning woman in Letterfanny mental asylum…one in her words…with good genes. She is Polish. There was an instant spark when our eyes met. I could tell she was interested.

She is single but the minute I asked her she turned off…it was bad timing…the nurse came to take her to get bloods. I'll let you know what happens when she comes back. She is so sexy. With a great ass!!!

20

SEX ON A MENTAL PATIENTS MIND

As we move into the new millennium there is a new kind of loving lol sex coming into the world. It will blow earths tiny miniscule mind how the orgasm is really meant to be! Our King Con knows how to blow! Don't you Con??…you're fucking right I do…when I'm not on these fucking evil castrating injections that stop ejaculation and erections. They are inhumane. I will put a stop to them worldwide!

I've just been woken up by an I.R.A man trying to be a Wildman like I used to be to wind the nurses up. I saw through his wonderfully intuitive conjured up from the depths of I.R.A intelligence plan. He knew I'd be waking up soon so with a loud voice and an argument with the staff…he has woken me up at 3.32am. About an hour before I normally get up. Little fucking piss ant foot soldier. I will break his heart and mind later on today in the tv room (AND I DID…lol). I'm getting excited now lol. He was shouting for a cup of coffee knowing that that's exactly what I'd be looking for when I got up. As I just told the nurses he was trying to head me off at the pass. Get his speak in and fuck it up for me. He also said lowly the dumb 60 year old fucking wankstain called Paddy Doherty from Inishowen as well…obviously one of our inbreeds...to the nurse "I bet that's Con woke up now... see him tholl (withstand) all night for a cigarette". He is one fucking plonker of a man. I've spent a bit of time in his company and he is a tit of a man. All made up now...he's one of our own.

I am addressing the most important thing in the world...SEX!!!

Sex is so important to every species on the planet. We need it to survivre. We need it to bon soir the concubines...we need it for our morning glory to bon matin la femmes. We need it all the fucking time. Don't get in the way of the natural course of life. I love women...I will be a one women man...at a time unless there is more of them.

As a mental patient...you will find the women are more voracious and have a bigger appetite for loving. We are so hungry for that orgasmic thrill that we get with even just a lustful glance of the eyes. I love to flirt. So does my earth wife Drea BUT Gotta is here on earth and I did not know that. Now I don't know what the hell is going on but Gotta is Sinead the trainee psychiatric nurse. She isn't even undercover. She is telling everyone who she is. I left my nails on the deck of my bathroom floor so they could be found just to see (under the instructions of Sachsion) what Gotta would say lol. She said I'm staying another day. I'm supposed to be going to another planet soon but the rules keep changing. Don't really give a fuck. Not sure what Gotta is after. She just said she wants me calmed down to the way I behave in Antibes then I'll take over Superyachting.

That is a bit of an impossibility. Gotta cannot be serious!!! John McEnroe said that, now I'm saying it...these people cannot compare to the breeding of the usual people I hang out with in Antibes. I will try but I'm putting up with no fucking shit!!!

I am so excited about going home. This world is dragging me down. Gotta just said not when I own a Superyacht. That will be exciting she said and her mixing me a Mojito every day...my perfect woman!

AN ODE TO GOTTA

She is the most wonderful human being on the planet and we know each other inside out. I love her laugh. I love her eyes. I love her smile and I know she has an amazing pussy on her lol.

The ira nurse Michael aka mickey just said as I was walking up the corridor of this special unit for the brave…"They'll calm that walk on you…they're putting a bullet in your knee!"

— Mickey the Nurse

See! I told you I was an alien…fuck the I.RA lol

Follow the Dealer
The South of France,
Is not for you,
You're not welcome,
My blade says two,
People on holiday,

As I think while I shave,
Oh la la...la la la la,
Oh how I'll behave,
When I meet them on their hols,
Men have they got balls,
I'll castrate,
Menstruate,
Bleed dry their wanderlust,
If I can,
Then I must,
The SoF is mine you CUNTS!!!
Stay the fuck away,
Or I will exact,
And will not retract,
Your vacationes aren't backed,
The psychiatric world is confined to the island of Ireland,
They're what you have discerned,
To all be mentally ill,
Cured by a pill,
And when they meet you on the outside,
All get a thrill,
I'm not from here,
I come from Antibes,
You all are a tree,
Without any leaves,
No patients left in me,
I HAVE CURED THEM ALL!!!
Stay away from my destination,
Or you will fall,
Into the abyss,
Of shit and piss,
You let them lie in,
When they're wild and free,

And can only see,
How a life full of fun is full of sin...
The I.R.A want to blow me up more!
The Ira are fucked,
The Jewish lives they've mucked,
Into their realm,
Of slime and deceit,
With no relief,
Of women that weep,
Sing a song of praise,
Happy are the dais,
Knowing is believing,
Consternation of relief,
Fabulosity of...fuck will they read anything!!!
When I go into yachting,
They said they'll blow up my yacht,
And I don't mean boast,
They aim to roast,
They are so bloody jealous,
Of my Royal British roots,
The Real I.R.A have everyone in cahoots,
They believe they rule the world,
Because the british sails they unfurled,
The I.R.B are involved as well,
They all need ECT'd,
It fucks up all of your memories,
To forget about the potatoe famine,
And all of their jealous greed,
The whole world will know,
How they screwed up my already fucked up life,
They even tried to force me,
To marry an ugly fat wife...just like them sos,
That hates fucking sex,

And won't do a tap,
And God forbid you like enjoying yourself,
Do drink and do drugs...she goes off her bleeding bap,
These little piss ants,
Are like psychiatric nurses,
They follow me like a dogsbody,
To the SoF and parade,
Their pseudo influential mind controlling head,
FUCKS,
attitude,
This is now over,
The patients will rise.
Tiocfaidh ar la!